Withdrawn Stock
Dorset Libraries

Withdrawn Stock
Dorset Libraries

Usborne
Stories
for
Little Children

Alice in Wonderland
& other stories

Usborne
Stories
for
Little Children

Alice in Wonderland
& other stories

Contents

The Town Mouse
and the Country Mouse   109

The Nutcracker

It was Christmas Eve.
The world was
covered in a crisp
blanket of snow.

Everything was dazzling white,
except for the golden light
that spilled out from
Clara's house.

Inside, a party was in full swing.
Clara stared out of the window...

She was waiting for something
magical to happen.

Suddenly,
the door burst open.

Merry Christmas, Clara!

It was her godfather.

"I've brought you a
wonderful present,"
he said.

To Clara,
This present isn't all
that it seems...
From your Godfather

"What can it be?"
wondered Clara, as she
lay in bed that night.

She was so excited,
she couldn't wait
to find out.

Clara ran downstairs...
and ripped off the
wrapping paper.

Inside was a
nutcracker toy.

Clara hugged him tight.
Then, with a yawn, she
curled up under the tree.
Soon, she was fast asleep.

Dong! Dong! The clock struck midnight. Clara woke with a start. There was a great *whooshing* sound.

The Christmas tree was rising up above her.

What's happening?

"Hello Clara," whispered a voice behind her.

"My nutcracker?" gasped Clara. He bowed. "I'm the Nutcracker Prince," he said.

15

"I've come to protect you.
The kitchen mice are plotting
to kidnap you."

He blew sharply on his whistle
and six soldiers marched
out of the toy box.

They were just in time. The kitchen
mice stormed out of
the shadows.

Ready! Aim! Fire!

The soldiers struck them down with lumps
of cheese and sprayed them with water.

Cheeeeese!

Help!

"Is cheese the best
you can do?" jeered
an evil voice.
It was the
Mouse King.

He whipped out his sword and lunged
at the Nutcracker Prince.

CLANG! CLASH!
went their swords.
"I must help!"
thought Clara.

She took off her slipper
and threw it.

Weeeeeeeeeeeeeeeeeee!

It whizzed through the
air and knocked the King out cold.

21

"You were brilliant!" said the Nutcracker Prince.
"Now we must celebrate."

He called for his reindeer and his magical,
golden sleigh. Clara and the Prince
climbed aboard.

They flew through an open window and into
the snow-filled sky.

The reindeer rode through the night.
Far below, Clara could see lollipop trees
and marshmallow flowers.

"Welcome to the Land of Sweets,"

announced the Prince.

They rode up to a marzipan castle,
decorated with all kinds of treats.

"I'm so glad you've come,"
said a dazzling fairy, dancing
out to greet them.

I am the Sugarplum Fairy.
Come inside and eat.

Clara and the Prince
sat down to a feast of
cookies and cakes
and candy swirls.

Then they watched
dances from around
the world.
Spinning Spanish dancers
clicked their castanets.

Arabian princesses
swirled...

...Chinese tea dancers
whirled...

...flower ballerinas twirled.

Clara watched, enchanted.

But the slow, soothing
music called her to sleep.
"It's time to go home,"
whispered the
Nutcracker Prince.

28

When Clara woke
up, she was under
the Christmas
tree once more
and the Prince
had gone.

"He's only a wooden toy!" cried Clara.
"It must have been a dream."

To Clara,
This present isn't all
that it seems...
From your Godfat

"Unless... unless... it was the magic
of Christmas Eve."

On the Farm

Can you imagine what it's like
to live on a farm?

As the sun comes up, the cockerel crows...

cock-a-doodle-doo

...and everyone in the
farmhouse begins to stir.

The cows come plodding
slowly down the lane.

Their warm breath
steams in the morning air.

Mooing and stomping their heavy feet,
the cows line up in the milking barn.

The farmer puts tubes
onto their pink udders...

...and their creamy milk
   is sucked into a cool tank.

A big tanker-truck rumbles into the farmyard.

The driver pumps the fresh milk
into the tanker and takes it away to be sold.

Next, it's time to feed the hens.

They peck-peck-peck
at the scattered corn.

Inside the little henhouse, nestled in the straw...

...are three warm, speckled eggs.

There are some new baby lambs over in the barn.
Two are sucking milk from their mother...

...and waggling their
woolly tails happily.

But there's no room
for the littlest one...

...so she has to be fed from a baby's bottle.
Soon, her tail starts waggling too.

Outside, the sheepdog is guiding
the sheep to a sunny meadow.

The farmer whistles
to tell him which way to run.

The dog crouches quietly at the gate
as the sheep trot through...

...and start to munch
on the long, green grass.

The tractor is chugging up and down
in the next field.

It's planting lots
of seeds in rows.

Hungry little birds
would like to eat the seeds...

...but the scarecrow
scares them all away.

Some plants are already growing
under a big, warm shelter.

There are tomato plants
(but no tomatoes yet)...

...and bean plants
with pretty flowers
(but not a single bean).

But there's plenty of lettuce
that's ready to eat.

The children pick
the biggest one
to take home.

As the sun sinks down behind the hills...

...the hens cluck sleepily
and go inside their henhouse.

The tractor comes chugging
across the field...

...and the farmer and his sheepdog
trudge back home.

Everyone kicks off their muddy boots
and scrambles inside.

It's the end of a very busy day.

Alice in Wonderland

Alice's sister was deep in her book
and Alice was feeling bored.

All at once, she saw a
White Rabbit
with a pocket watch.

"Whoever heard of a rabbit with a pocket – or a watch?" thought Alice curiously...

...and she followed him

down

    into

       his

         hole.

D
o
w
n
D
o
w
n
D
o
w
n

Alice thought the hole would
never end, until she landed –
with a BUMP.

She was in a hall, looking onto a
beautiful garden. But she was much
too big to fit through the door.

Sunlight glinted on a glass bottle in the hall.

"Falling down holes is thirsty work,"
thought Alice. She took a great big gulp...

...and shrank to the size of a mouse.
Now she could fit through the door!

She was walking past a curly table leg
when she saw an
inviting cake.

"Eat me!"
it said.

Eat Me

Alice bit into the sticky icing... and shot up so quickly, her head hit the ceiling.

Now she was much too tall.

Alice started to cry.

Huge, salty tears splashed onto the floor.

Just then, the White Rabbit ran past in a fluster.

"Oh my ears and whiskers, I'll be late!"

he gasped, dropping his fan.

Alice scooped it up...
and shrank again.

With a **splish** she tumbled into her salty lake of tears.

Peculiar creatures crowded around her.

"Swim for the shore!" they cried, so Alice swam.

"Shall I tell you a story?" she said, as they dried off. "My cat—"

"CAT?" they squawked and hurried away in a scurry of claws and a flurry of wings.

Left all alone, Alice wandered along until she met a grumpy-looking caterpillar.

"Who are you?" he said.

"I don't know," sighed Alice. "I keep growing and shrinking and it's all very confusing."

"Try eating some of my mushroom," said the caterpillar.

Alice nibbled a piece.

In a blink, the caterpillar vanished and a grinning cat appeared. Alice was baffled – and totally lost. "Where do I go now?" she asked.

"*That* way for the Hatter and *that* way for the March Hare," said the cat.

Alice decided to visit the Hare and found the Hatter there too. They were drinking tea and talking nonsense.

"Why is a raven like a writing desk?"

Alice got more and
more confused.

"This is the stupidest tea party
ever!" she said, running off.

"What party? Who are you?" snapped a voice. Alice had run slap-bang-wham into the Queen of Hearts.

"We're about to play a game," said the King, before Alice could answer. "Won't you join us?"

It was the strangest game Alice had ever seen.

Anyone who played badly was dragged away by the Queen's guards.

"Everyone to court!" said the Queen, all of a sudden.
Alice followed behind but she was growing again.
"Off with her head!" shouted the Queen.

"Nonsense!" said Alice.

"You're nothing but a pack of cards!" she added.

Suddenly, everything whirled into the air,
spinning her around, faster and faster.

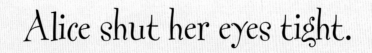

Alice shut her eyes tight.

When she opened them again,
all the cards had gone...

and she was back at the
top of the rabbit hole.

"Curiouser and curiouser," said Alice,
and she went home for tea.

The Snow Queen

Long, long ago,

and even further away,

lived two best friends, Gerda and Kay.

In all the world, no two friends were as close.

One crisp winter's day, Kay was crunching through the snow when he saw a twinkling snowflake.

It grew larger...

and larger...

until, suddenly, it turned into a woman, dressed in a sparkling white cloak.

The next second, she was gone.

The following afternoon, Kay was with Gerda when - ow! - a sharp speck of ice flew into his eye. From that moment, everything changed.

Kay began teasing Gerda and ripping up all her precious flowers. Then he made fun of people in the street.

As each day passed, he grew more and more horrible.

"Whatever's happened to Kay?" Gerda asked her grandmother.
Gerda's grandmother shook her head sadly and sighed.
"I think he's been enchanted by the Snow Queen," she said.

After a while, Kay ignored Gerda altogether. He only wanted to play outside in the snow.

His cheeks glowed and his eyes shone.

He never seemed to notice the cold.

On the coldest day of the winter, the Snow Queen came for Kay.
In a daze, he caught hold of her sleigh.

She commanded her snow-white horse
in a voice spikier than icicles.

HOME!

And they flew from the market square, Kay clinging on behind.

The Snow Queen took Kay far, far away, to her palace of ice in the frozen north.

Kay grew colder, and colder, and colder...
so cold, he might have been carved from ice himself.

Week after week, he sat still as a snowman,
trapped in a room made from blocks of ice.

Soon, he completely forgot Gerda and everything in his old life.

But Gerda didn't forget Kay.

As the flowers started to bloom,
she set off to look for him.

First, she followed
the winding river.

When the river ran out, she left her boat and walked.
She walked for days and days...

...until, lost and alone in a
forest, she finally stopped.
A glossy black crow
hopped up to her.
"Caaaaw," he croaked.
"What's wrong?"

"I'm looking for my friend," she said.
"The Snow Queen stole him."
"A queen?" croaked the crow.
"Perhaps she's taken him to the
palace by the lake. Caaaaaaw.
I'll show you."

He led Gerda through sleeping halls,
where royal dreams glided past.
"Try the robbers' castle," they
whispered. "Take the golden
coach outside."

The robbers' castle stood high on a hill,
stark against the sky.

Following a moonlit
path, the golden coach
rattled its way to
the top.

Inside the castle, Gerda told her story again.

"The Snow Queen lives in the frozen north," said a robber girl. "My reindeer can take you."

The robber girl watched them go, waving until Gerda and her reindeer were out of sight.

They had a long, hard journey ahead.

100

The air turned cold and stung Gerda's face like hail.
Her face went numb but still they kept going.

At last, towering in the distance, she saw the Snow Queen's
glittering palace of ice.

In a whirl of snowflakes, the Queen's guards sprang at Gerda.

As Gerda cried out,
her breath formed
into misty angels.

Silently, they
swooped down and
attacked the palace guards.

Gerda ran into the palace calling for Kay.

She put her hand over his frozen
heart and it began to thaw.
A warm tear melted the speck of
ice in Kay's eye and trickled down
his cheek. "Gerda?" he whispered.

Kay jumped up, sending blocks of ice flying.
The Snow Queen could only watch in
icy fury, as Gerda and Kay fled, leaving her
chilly palace forever.

Back at home, Gerda's grandmother was overjoyed to see them. "I can't believe you escaped the Snow Queen!" she cried, over and over again.

And she hugged them both tightly, as if she'd never, ever let them go.

The Town Mouse and the Country Mouse

In among the waving grasses,

lies a little brown country mouse, fast asleep.
His name is Pipin.

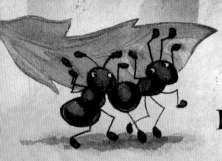

He dreams of crunchy seeds
and juicy red strawberries.

Every evening Pipin
pattered home

to his little house
in the leafy hedge.

Then, one cold winter's day, there was
a RAT-A-TAT-TAT at his door.

"Pipin!" cried a voice.
It was Toby Town Mouse, come to stay.

"Oh my whiskers!" cried Pipin.
He rushed to his pantry for his best nuts and berries.

"Is this all you have?"
asked Toby Town Mouse.

"In town we eat like kings.
I think you'd better come and stay with me."

The mice scampered to the station
early next morning.

The train trundled in with
a snort and a shriek.

"It's HUGE!" gasped Pipin.
"It's like a **big**
red
beast."

They wriggled inside a man's
green bag and were lifted aboard. Then...

Chugga-chugga-chugga. Choo! Choo!
They were off!

Pipin gazed out of the window,
at trees waving their branches.

Then there were no trees at all –
just tall buildings that touched the sky.

"At last!" cried Toby, sniffing the air. "We're here!"

Hurry up, Pipin!

They ran out of the station
onto a busy street.

"Help!" squeaked Pipin, dodging
in and out of stamping feet.

"This is it," said Toby, proudly pointing his paw. "My house."
They crept through a crack under the blue front door.

Toby led Pipin down under the floor,
up secret stairs behind the walls

and into a splendid dining hall.

The mice nibbled and gnawed

and scooped cream with their paws,

until they were perfectly full.

Zzzz

Hic!

They woke with a start as the table shook.

"MY dinner time!"
purred the kitchen cat.

Mmmmm...
Juicy little mice.

"Run!" squeaked Toby.

The mice darted
this way
and that.

Pounce! Pounce!
went the hungry cat.

She swiped at Pipin
with her pointy claws.

Quick, Pipin! Into this hole.

Pipin ran.

The cat leaped...

...and missed.

"Curses!" she hissed.

"Oh my whiskers," said Pipin, mopping his brow.
"I want to go home."

Oh! Why?

"This town life is too much for me."

Toby took Pipin to the station
and waved goodbye.

Pipin gazed again
as tall buildings
flashed quickly
past his eyes.

In the starry dark, Pipin
finally reached his hedge.

He sniffed the cold, sweet air and smiled.

Then he snuggled down
in his soft, mossy bed.

"This is the life for me," Pipin said.

"And this is the life for me," said Toby.

The Nutcracker started life as a story, but in 1892, a Russian composer named Tchaikovsky turned it into a ballet. It is now performed all over the world, especially at Christmas time.

On the Farm tells the captivating story of a day in the life of a farm. It was written with help from Rupert Aker at the Soil Association, who was full of useful information about farming.

Alice in Wonderland was originally called Alice's Adventures Underground. Charles Lutwidge Dodgson, a vicar and teacher, made up the story to amuse his young friend Alice Liddell during a boat trip. It was published in 1865 with a new title, Alice's Adventures in Wonderland, and a new name for the author – Lewis Carroll.

The Snow Queen was written by Hans Christian Andersen. Born in Denmark in 1805, he was the son of a poor shoemaker. He left home at the age of fourteen to seek his fortune, and became famous all over the world as a writer of fairy tales.

The Town Mouse and the Country Mouse

is based on one of Aesop's Fables, a collection of stories first told in Ancient Greece around 4,000 years ago. The stories always have a "moral" (a message or lesson) at the end.

Designed by Laura Parker, Katarina Dragoslavic
Andrea Slane and Caroline Spatz.
Cover designed by Lenka Hrehova.
Edited by Jenny Tyler, Lesley Sims and Gillian Doherty.

This edition first published in 2014 by Usborne Publishing Ltd,
83-85 Saffron Hill, London EC1N 8RT, England.
www.usborne.com Copyright © 2014, 2007 Usborne Publishing Ltd.
The name Usborne and the devices ♀ 🎈 are Trade Marks of Usborne Publishing Ltd.
All rights reserved. No part of this publication may be reproduced, stored in a retrieval system,
or transmitted in any form or by any means, electronic, mechanical, photocopying,
recording or otherwise, without the prior permission of the publisher. UE.